The Killing Frost

February 26, 2000

To Tina,
What a special gift to have gained you as a friend! Thank you for your support, and for being such a very special person!

Much love,
Lynn Rice King

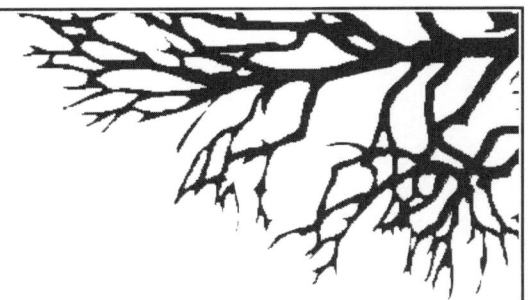

The Killing Frost

Lynn Rice King

Pentland Press, Inc.
England·USA·Scotland

PUBLISHED BY PENTLAND PRESS, INC.
5122 Bur Oak Circle, Raleigh, North Carolina 27612
United States of America
(919)782-0281

ISBN: 1-57197-111-4
Library of Congress Catalog Card Number 98-065630
Copyright 1998 Lynn Rice King
All rights reserved, which includes the right to reproduce this
book or portions thereof in any form whatsoever except as
provided by the U.S. Copyright Law.
Printed in the United States of America

This book is dedicated, with love, to my children: Carter, Ellery, and Clare.

Table of Contents

Chapter One 1

Chapter Two 11

Chapter Three 15

Chapter Four 23

Chapter Five 27

Chapter Six 31

Chapter Seven 39

Chapter Eight 51

Chapter Nine 55

Chapter Ten 63

Chapter Eleven 65

Chapter Twelve 69

"I can do all things through him who strengthens me." Phil. 4:13

Chapter One

SHE LIKED TO walk in the mornings, at dawn actually. It was still dark when she stepped outside her front door, but by the time she reached her destination—the highest hill in the neighborhood and the midpoint of her walk—the sun would have presented itself, sometimes sneakily seeming to appear as if from nowhere, and sometimes majestically crowning the mountain tops amidst a blushing background. Yet always it appeared, and the certainty of this sentinel in the sky was a comfort to Vera.

Vera viewed the earth as the garment of the Living God and gained resolve to be a further reflection of his love by feeding off this primary level of beauty extended through his creation.

As a child, Vera had considered the creation story found in the Book of Genesis to be problematic. It seemed too simple; it was boring, like reading a nursery rhyme that you already knew by heart. There were still so many questions it left unanswered.

But now she appreciated the scriptural creation story on a different level. She loved it because of, not in spite of, its fundamental simplicity. God created the earth: the sea, the sky, the stars, the plants, and every living creature, culminating in human life as a result of his love for humankind. Vera now used this creation, this beauty, this evidence of the Creator's love as a power source. She gained energy from appreciating this beauty and was then able to radiate love, energy, and a sense of beauty to others.

Her vocation was director of religious education at the largest Protestant church downtown. Her career choice was a reaction to the love she received from God and which she wished to transmit to others.

Paradoxically, reflecting her Creator's love often put Vera at odds with other church members whose motivations were more self-serving.

Besides serving the purpose of recharging her spiritual batteries, Vera walked in the early morning hours as a matter of convenience, also; for once she returned home, showered, and dressed, her day became a jumble of overlapping activities.

Vera's day at the church started early and often seemed endless. Even before leaving her house in the morning, she would usually get one or two calls from members of the congregation needing schedule reminders, wanting to share program ideas, or notifying her of someone who had been hospitalized during the night.

In cases of pastoral care emergencies, Vera would eclipse her usual schedule of preparing religious study programming in order to visit with someone who was ill, or had a family in need.

It was, in fact, at a social event stemming from a spiritual event that Vera first met him.

She was at a wedding reception at the local country club. The wedding itself had been beautiful: the flowers, the music, the dress, and the girl were all lovely and well-coordinated. Vera pushed aside any misgivings over the "better or worse" portion of the ceremony; it seemed from the high rate of failed marriages that the bride and groom only expected the "better" circumstances to result from their own union, and as a result didn't feel the need to stick around and support the other through any personal 'worse' scenarios he or she might encounter. But Vera traded in these thoughts of doubt for hope on this day of celebration.

Vera had gone outside to get some fresh air and take a break from the wedding reception crowd when she first saw him.

He was standing at the poolside patio and talking, or rather seemed to be listening, to a small group of men who had evidently gone outside to smoke cigars.

He was the most physically beautiful person Vera had ever seen. If he were devoid of color, he could have been mistaken for a poolside marble statue of a Greek warrior god, Vera thought to herself.

But color was what seemed to animate his chiseled features and make him even more physically exquisite. His skin was olive in complexion, and his thick dark hair almost seemed to taunt Vera's fingers into losing themselves in its luster. Vera couldn't make out the color of his eyes and felt compelled to get closer to him in an effort to learn more.

He looked bored. As he listened to the other men, he gently tossed an apple that he must have picked up from the centerpiece of the fruit and cheese tray sitting on the nearby buffet table.

The rhythmic up and down motion of the fruit caught Vera's eye as she descended the steps that led to the country club's poolside patio.

Vera was mesmerized by the measured motion of the apple being pitched precariously into the air and then caught in calculated rhythm, only to be tossed again. The moments seemed to be measured by the slapping sound of the fruit connecting with the stranger's hand.

He turned his head to look at her.

The apple fell to the ground, breaking Vera's trance.

She feebly smiled as her mind raced in an effort to determine the situation. How long had she been standing there staring? How awkward did she seem? Should she say "hello?" Should she turn and walk back up to the clubhouse?

"Hello," he said gracefully, striding toward her. "I don't believe we've met before. My name is Rafe."

"Hi," she smiled as she took his hand.

They stood silent for a moment. Vera glanced at the apple now laying on the ground.

"I'm afraid I've spoiled it," he said, following her gaze. "I never was very good at juggling."

Vera smiled again, guessing that she looked pretty stupid. She still couldn't think of anything to say, even though her senses were whirling.

"Well," she finally said, struggling to regain composure, "I guess I should return to the party."

"I wish you would stay. A party is wherever you make it." He looked down in embarrassment over his remark and then slowly raised his head, gently locking his beautiful dark eyes into her fair blue ones. "I haven't even learned your name."

"I'm sorry; I'm Vera. Vera Adamson."

"Vera—that's an unusual name."

"I'm named after my great-grandmother. I read in a baby name book once that it means 'truth.'"

"Truth. How beautiful."

"Rafe isn't a very common name either."

"No, it isn't. I don't know where it came from. I was adopted as an infant and it's the name my birth mother wanted me to have. That's one of the reasons I'm here visiting."

"In pursuit of your birth mother?"

"Something like that. It's a complicated story." He smiled smoothly and changed the subject. "Anyway, I'm a newcomer to the South, and feel as if I'm very much the foreigner. What can you tell me about this town? Are you from here?"

"My family has lived in the South for generations, as far back as anyone can remember. I grew up here in Mountain Ridge and have lived here most of my life. I consider it home. It's a friendly town once you get used to it."

"Maybe you could help me with the 'getting used to it' part. Mountain Ridge seems to be a charming town; I'd love to hear more about it, as well as about the people who live here. Would you be able to join me for a drink and tell me more?"

Vera looked at him. Rafe was absolutely the most gorgeous man she had ever met. She couldn't believe he looked so vulnerable, as if his hopes would be crushed if she turned him down. If he had known her better, he would have realized that she always took time to visit with anyone who felt the need to talk or share. She smiled radiantly, her eyes sparkling.

"I think I can manage that," she playfully teased.

They walked together to the poolside bar, where she asked for a glass of wine and he ordered a beer. He lightly put his hand on her back as he guided her toward a glider, a large swinging chair. He brushed off the seat and then majestically presented it to her with a grand gesture, as if she were a princess ascending her throne and he were a mere footman.

They sat, gently swinging, as they talked and watched the sun set over the golf course.

"So what is it that you do in this beautiful town of Mountain Ridge?" Rafe asked.

"I'm a director of religious education at the First Church of God. It's the old gray stone church in the downtown historical district. You may have seen it."

"Yes, I did notice it. It's a beautiful building."

Vera nodded her head in agreement. "It's a fun place to work for the most part; very creative and challenging."

Rafe eyed Vera's short, sleeveless, silk sheath dress that whispered against the curves of her body. Her long blonde hair was styled in a French twist. She was wearing high-heeled pumps and a long strand of pearls. "You certainly don't look like a Sunday School teacher," he said.

"I know. Sometimes I feel as if I don't fit in anywhere."

"What do you mean?" Rafe asked.

"Well, when I first meet people at secular events, like meeting you this evening, they often seem uncomfortable when they learn that I work for a church."

"Do I look uncomfortable to you?" Rafe asked.

Vera looked at him. He was sitting back in the glider, gently rocking with the swing's motion. He took a sip from his beer, a soft smile playing about his lips.

"No, you don't look uncomfortable, Rafe," Vera responded. "But I get the impression that there's not much about you that is typical."

His smile broadened. "You're a fast learner," he said, raising his beer in a mock salute. "Or maybe you understand me so well because we're so similar."

"Oh," Vera said as she settled in to the swing, looking at Rafe while returning his remarks, "Are you a loner too?"

"You might say that," he said, taking another sip of beer. "But tell me, Miss Adamson, surely you must feel that you fit in at the church. I mean, it is your chosen profession."

Vera looked contemplative and took a sip of her wine. "I'm not so sure. I mean, I know I drive all the older women at the church crazy by the way I dress. Usually they consider my attire too informal to suit their tastes, but it's more comfortable for me when I'm running up and down the church stairs all day, or lifting boxes, or decorating bulletin boards." She paused, straightening and then bending her legs while swinging in the glider. "I suppose I must admit, however, that I almost always wear my skirts too short. I guess I'm a rebel at heart."

"You chose a strange line of work to be a rebel."

She smiled. "Well, maybe 'rebel' is too strong a word. I do push the envelope, though, as far as defining spirituality."

"How so?" he asked.

"Well, for instance, I don't like the fact that people often define a person's level of spirituality by the manner in which they dress. So, I guess I sometimes dress to raise a few eyebrows in a hope to make them reassess their standards." Vera replied.

"Interesting." Rafe took another sip of his beer. "So did you always know that you wanted to go into church work?"

"No. I majored in English in college, but even then I knew I wanted to do something that would be helpful to others. You know, make the world a better place."

Rafe smiled and nodded his head. "So, are you still such an optimist?"

Vera continued to glide in the chair, back and forth, while she considered the question. "Yes and no. Originally, I expected to be working in a friendly, nurturing, and supportive environment. I assumed that everyone who walked through the door would share in the love of God and in the need to uplift others as a result of that love."

"And you were wrong?" he asked.

"Let's just say that I was very naive." She took a sip of her wine. "I don't mean to downplay the fact that there are a lot of kind, caring people that make up our, or any, congregation. I've certainly witnessed many occasions when church members bond together and offer their prayers and helping hands to one another during times of personal crisis." Vera seemed reflective.

"But the other times?"

"The goodness of these people, as well as the Biblical teachings we study, promotes a climate of acceptance and compassion—the perfect sanctuary for those in need of exerting power or influence over others."

"You mean they take advantage of others' goodness?" Rafe increased the pace of the swinging chair. "Those hypocrites! Now I remember why I stopped going to church."

"'Yep, the church is full of hypocrites. You should come join us some Sunday. There's always room for one more."

He looked at her sharply.

She smiled. "I'm sorry. But I feel that if we were to each study our lives, what we believe, what we say, and what we do, then we would discover that we're all hypocrites. People are imperfect, but at least in a church environment most of them are struggling toward the standard of Godly perfection."

"Do you honestly think that you have to walk inside a church building in order to improve yourself?" Rafe asked defensively.

"No, not at all. As a matter of fact, the latest statistics show that the majority of American believers now lie outside the church's domain."

"They admit to believing in God and yet they don't attend church? Why is that?" Rafe asked.

Rafe had hit upon Vera's area of interest. "No one seems to know for sure, but obviously people's spiritual needs are no longer being fulfilled by the traditional church. I've given this trend a lot of thought, and it seems to me that a broadening definition and sense of spirituality has evolved over the ages, but the church, since the sixteenth century Protestant Reformation, has failed to evolve in tandem. As a result, prayers are still spoken in King James English, and creeds, which do not always echo the sentiments, beliefs, or concerns of the believers, are asked to be repeated aloud at weekly worship."

"So, do you consider the church to be an outdated institution?"

"I think it's got some catching up to do, but change, in a spiritual context, is always considered to be threatening. It sometimes seems as if the mainline Protestant churches are ignoring the spiritual needs of the majority in order to protect and preserve their own identity."

"But what about the fundamentalist churches? They're growing, aren't they?" Rafe asked.

"Yes, and they do seem to give more attention to the spiritual needs of their members, but the fundamentalist churches I've attended seem to neglect the intellect—the thinking, questioning faith process of their members—in order to feed them on a more emotional level. Their resolve and enthusiasm seems to diminish once they leave the security of their congregational corps."

Rafe nodded his head, taking all of this in. "I can see you have given this a lot of thought. And yet, even with all of these problems, you still want to continue your work in the church?'"

Vera stared ahead at the stars that punctuated the dark night sky. "It's no longer what I do; it's who I am."

Chapter Two

THE NEXT MORNING, at church, Vera was surprised, and pleased, to see him again.

She was distributing Bibles to the children in the front pews before the worship service began. It seemed almost amazing to Vera how the Bibles would disappear from the front seats from one week to the next. Vera assumed that the children must take the Bibles with them when they returned to sit with their parents following the Children's Sermon.

As she was handing a Bible to little Sarah Brinkley, Rafe walked in the back door of the church. Vera was so surprised to see him, and so absorbed by his presence that she dropped the heavy book, which Sarah had not yet tightly grasped.

He approached her.

Vera straightened and smiled, putting on her best church greeting face, which she hoped didn't look out of the ordinary.

"Hi," he smiled.

"Hi," she smiled back. "What a nice surprise."

"Well, it was a little difficult getting up and going this morning. A new friend kept me up pretty late last night."

Vera blushed faintly. "I enjoyed our visit."

"Me too. That's why I'm here today. I couldn't wait to see you again."

The organ music started.

"That's the prelude. I need to take my seat next to the children so that I can deliver the Children's Sermon during the service. Maybe I'll see you later."

"I'd like that," he smiled as she shuffled off to find her seat.

Following the worship service, Rafe found Vera in Fellowship Hall, her back facing him as she visited with some of the parishioners. He approached her from behind and gently placed his hand on her shoulder. She turned to meet him.

"Oh, hi, Rafe. Did you enjoy the service?"

"I got something out of it. It did leave a few unanswered questions in my mind, however."

Vera nodded her head. "That's the mark of a good sermon. You're supposed to turn those questions over in your mind and heart throughout the week as you progress in your faith journey."

He looked at her, intrigued. "Please continue."

The couple with whom Vera had been visiting quietly left the two young people alone to talk.

"The people who have questions in church don't scare me as much as the ones who seem to have all the answers," she chuckled. "Questions are a natural part of faith development. We are like children asking a parent about a world we can't yet comprehend."

"And do you always receive answers to your questions?"

"Sometimes, but the process almost always requires personal involvement—you must first be open to receiving the answer, even if it's not the one you hoped for, and then you must pray, study, and consider the different perspectives and implications of your question."

"And then you receive your answer?"

"Not always. That's where the faith part comes in. Sometimes the answer is that there is no answer and that's when you're required to trust in God."

"Pardon me for saying this, but that sounds kind of like a cop-out. When you can't understand something, you just place it under God's jurisdiction. That seems to be a neat and tidy, not to mention simplistic, solution."

"It may seem neat and tidy, and even simplistic, but it's certainly not easy," Vera responded. "We are so caught up in control issues in today's world that we hate to relinquish any portion of our lives to anyone else."

"That's a pretty broad-sweeping statement," Rafe remarked.

"Well, think about it. So many people in today's society consider themselves to be from dysfunctional families. We then grow up, marry, and divorce. It seems as if we can't trust anyone, so the concept of God, a seemingly archaic perception of an invisible entity who supposedly loves us, even though there's not much evidence of that love in our day-to-day disappointments and anxiety-filled lives, seems easy to dismiss as a myth, a fairy tale."

"Good point. So why are we here?" Rafe gestured to the church walls surrounding them.

Vera reached over to a nearby urn and began filling two cups of coffee. "Because as hard as we try, we can't deny God's presence. Someone or something created this world, and when we take the time and energy, we can discover that it's filled with a lot of beauty. You can't observe the first flowers of spring, or the face of a newborn child, or the sun rising over a mountain or setting over an ocean without being filled with a sense of awe and respect for the Creator."

"But what if 'God' is just a childish explanation for creation, an unexplainable occurrence?"

Vera handed Rafe a filled cup. "Then why do we always turn to him in our time of need? It seems almost instinctive. I doubt you'd find an atheist among the passengers aboard a crashing plane."

"Maybe they're just trying to cover all the bases."

"Maybe," Vera reflected as she sipped her coffee, "and maybe we need to abandon our adult fears and skepticism and pragmatism in order to develop the simple beautiful faith of a child that can perceive the sophistication of her Creator without having to understand it."

"But that still doesn't answer the most basic question I had during today's church service," Rafe said, grinning coyly.

Vera laughed, recognizing his playfulness. "And what might that be?" she asked with a raised eyebrow.

He bent down close to her face and whispered huskily, "I was wondering if I might be able to convince the church's pretty director of religious education to have lunch with me."

Vera blushed and glanced about the emptying Fellowship Hall.

"Did you have other plans?" Rafe pressed.

"Well, no, but . . ."

"Then it's a date. You finish doing what you have to do here, and I'll go get us a table at the Chinese restaurant I saw down the street. Come join me when you can."

He gave her arm a gentle squeeze and was gone.

Chapter Three

"NO, MOTHER, IT'S nothing serious. He's just someone I met at the Meyers' wedding."

Vera was standing at the sink in her parents' kitchen, helping prepare the salad for their traditional Sunday family dinner.

"'Nothing serious.' And you had lunch with him today?" Vera's mother looked skeptical.

"He's new in town. I don't think he knows many people. Maybe he's just a little lonely."

"A little lonely, my foot! Vera, this man is not one of those homeless kittens you used to drag home. Now tell me what you know about him. What's he doing here anyway?"

"He's here on family business." Vera answered evasively.

"Family business? What kind of family business?"

"I'm not sure." Vera hated to reveal personal information about another person, and was defensive of Rafe and his right to privacy, especially in the face of her mother's inquisition. But truth be told, Vera realized she didn't know very much about the dark stranger who had entered her life. She and Rafe had spent hours together talking, and yet he had revealed very little about himself. Vera made a mental note to try to learn more about him—if she ever saw him again.

"Humph! Well what does he do, Vera? Surely you know that?" her mother asked, not a little sarcastically. She was enjoying the role of being the protective mother hen.

"Yes, Mother, he's in sales." Vera responded, relieved to at last have an answer.

"Sales? What does he sell? Is that why he's here in town?"

Vera pushed the carrot scrapings down the garbage disposal and turned it on, hoping the noise would drown out her answer, or at least any argument her mother might have. "I'm not sure," she said meekly.

Mrs. Adamson put down the place mats and cloth napkins she had been retrieving from the sideboard and walked over to her daughter. She gently cupped her daughter's face in her hands and raised it to her own. "It's okay, sweetheart," she said softly as she smoothed Vera's hair back from her face. "At least tell me where he's from."

"I don't know, Mama," Vera said, trying to keep the tears from her eyes and her voice strong and level. "I think he's from somewhere up north. He's mentioned New York City once or twice. I told you, he travels quite a bit."

The two women looked down at the floor. Not knowing who someone was, who his people were, where he was from, was an inexcusable offense when you lived in the South. Maybe it hearkened back to the post-Civil War era, when someone you didn't know was liable to steal you blind. Maybe it resulted from rural communities in which everyone knew everybody and a stranger was a rarity. Regardless, tradition ruled that Southerners be proud of their heritage, whatever it may be; it was something that you stated outright as soon as you met someone. It was your tag, your identity, something that followed you around and that you passed on to your children.

Beth Adamson turned and began selecting silverware from a nearby drawer in order to set the table.

Vera tried to strengthen her position. "Mother, I told you, I've just met the man."

Mrs. Adamson turned and looked strongly at her daughter, pointing a butter knife for emphasis. "Now you listen to me, Vera. You're not a little girl any more. You be careful of this stranger before he steals your heart."

The reception Vera got from others was different. Everyone was curious about Rafe and his interest in Vera.

"What's he like?" Vera's best friend, Maggy, asked. "I mean besides being the best-looking man alive."

"He's not 'like' anything. I've told you I really don't know him that well."

"Come on, do your old married friend a favor. My life's so boring, I have to live vicariously through you. I've heard he's rich."

"I wouldn't know. I've only talked to him a few times, and he hasn't said much about himself. I'm just being nice to the new guy in town who doesn't know many people. You wouldn't be reacting this way if Rafe were some older lady who could use a friend."

"Oh, right!" Maggy snorted.

Vera looked hurt.

"Look, buddy, you might be trying to fool yourself with that 'just being a friend' line, but please don't expect me to believe it. Not to say that you aren't friendly to those in need, but you'd have to be made of stone for Rafe not to affect you. I get goose bumps just thinking about him!"

"He is handsome," Vera acknowledged, and then smiled at her friend. "Do you really think he might be interested in me?"

Days passed before Vera heard from Rafe again. She had tried not to think of him, but it seemed that the more time passed without seeing him or hearing from him, the more thoughts of him entered her mind.

She tried to convince herself that the arguments she had given her mother were correct after all. Rafe was lonely, new in town, and she had been a friendly diversion. She steeled herself to the fact that she would probably never see him again; her subconscious hopes that he had found her to be someone special had been just that—vain hopes.

She was at her desk in the church office, trying to mentally focus on preparing for a Bible Study class when he walked through her door.

"Well hello, stranger." Vera smiled. "I was beginning to think I'd never see you again," she said.

Rafe winced dramatically. "I'm so sorry, Vera. I was called out of town unexpectedly. I didn't even have a chance to phone you and explain."

She shuffled papers on her desk and tried to act as if she hadn't noticed, as if his sudden departure had been of no consequence to her.

"Please let me make up for my rudeness. What's the nicest restaurant in town?"

Vera looked down at her paperwork, trying to act nonchalant. "I guess that would be La Mirabelle."

"Great. Let's go there. Tonight. I'll pick you up around seven o'clock."

"Tonight? I'm not sure I can make it." She didn't like the fact that he was obviously taking her for granted.

"Please? It would mean so much to me." He looked uncomfortable at not getting his way, and then calmly added, "Vera, please pardon my tactless behavior. I don't seem to have been myself lately. It would really mean a lot for me to go to the nicest restaurant in town, with the most beautiful girl in town." He looked softly into her eyes. "I've missed you."

Vera returned his gaze. "I'll see you at seven."

Vera opened her door promptly at seven o'clock and inhaled deeply. He looked like a vision standing in her doorway. His hair was combed back and shone like blue-black satin, exposing the high ridge of his cheekbones and accentuating his dark-fringed eyes. His starched white shirt, which peeked beneath his dinner jacket, contrasted dramatically with the golden smoothness of his skin. In his hands he held a bouquet of red rosebuds, which he presented to her.

"Are you ready?" he asked. "You look beautiful."

Vera looked down at her pale blue linen dress, which was far from new. "I guess so," she smiled self-consciously.

At dinner they talked quietly about little things; the weather, how he was settling into town, the people he was meeting. Vera didn't ask, and he didn't offer to say how long he would be living amongst them.

The candle on their table burned between them as they spoke.

Rafe reached over and gently covered Vera's hand, which rested on the table, with his own. Vera marveled at how his large dark hand completely covered her pale delicate one. She hoped she wasn't trembling.

"You truly are beautiful, Vera. I hope tonight has been special for you, because I want it to be the first of many that we share together."

"My life is just beginning," Vera thought to herself. She felt as if she would always be joined to this man who now clasped her hand; that her life, her future, indeed her very soul would be linked to this man who had touched her heart. She felt like a princess who, because she had endured life's hardships admirably, always holding onto hope and a belief in goodness and the perseverance of truth, was being rewarded, even rescued, by this handsome dark prince.

"Life is like a fairy tale after all," Vera thought to herself. Her eyes gazed openly into Rafe's and reflected the flickering flame between them.

The next day they met again. Rafe had asked Vera to decide where they should have lunch, and said that he'd pick her up at the church around noon.

Vera was waiting in Fellowship Hall when he entered.

"Hi. Are you ready to go?" he asked.

"I sure am," she said as she began walking toward the door.

"Where are we going?" he asked.

"Just a little place on the outskirts of town that I know of. I'll drive."

"Okay," he said as he followed her out the door.

It took several minutes for them to reach their destination. Rafe was awestruck by the beauty of the little town called Mountain Ridge. The town itself was nestled between the mountains that gave the town its name. As Vera negotiated the many hilltops and curves, Rafe was impressed by the acres of virgin forest that boasted such an abundance of colorful foliage.

"Well, here we are."

Rafe looked around. They had stopped at a grassy area that sloped down beside a large lake. Beautiful water, so glassy that it reflected the clouds floating overhead, stretched as far as he could see. The lake was fringed with trees, and there was no evidence of human civilization.

"This is quite a restaurant," he remarked. "I hope you called ahead to reserve our seating."

Vera laughed as she opened her trunk and removed a picnic basket and a small ice chest. She handed Rafe a blanket and the ice chest, and walked toward the lake shore. Rafe spread out the blanket and Vera unpacked their lunch.

As they began nibbling on their food, Vera stared at the shimmering lake and the trees beyond. She sighed deeply, "This is one of my very favorite places on earth."

"I can see why," Rafe said as he took her hand in his own. "Thank you for sharing it with me."

He watched her intently as she absorbed the beauty of her environment. "You know, I think your eyes are as blue as the water."

She turned to look at him and then looked down at the blanket.

"I have always loved water. It has such a calming effect." She looked at him again. "I've always lived near a lake or river. I guess I've gotten kind of spoiled."

"You're lucky. Most people don't have access to such unblemished beauty." He touched a strand of her hair. "Your hair is the same color as the golden shimmers of the sun on the lake."

Vera looked back at the lake, embarrassed. "Next you're going to tell me my skin is as green as the grass."

"Hi, Beth, how are you today?"

Mrs. Adamson was raking leaves in the front yard and her neighbor, Mary Ann Bridges, hailed her as she walked by.

"I'm fine, Mary Ann. How are you?" Beth looked up, wiping the sweat from her forehead with the back of her garden glove.

"I'm great. Just out for some exercise on this beautiful day," Mary Ann said as she approached her neighbor. "How's that daughter of yours?"

"Vera? She seems to be fine." Mrs. Adamson straightened her back, getting comfortable for what she now knew was to be a neighborly visit.

"I heard she's been keeping company with that new fellow in town. What's his name?"

"Rafe?"

"That's right. Are they getting serious?"

"Who knows? You know children rarely tell their parents anything."

"Well, Betty MacPherson said she saw the two of them going into La Mirabelle Restaurant the other night."

"Oh?" said Beth, refusing to acknowledge whether or not this was new information to her.

"Uh huh. Betty said she saw this beautiful silver Mercedes pull up to the restaurant, and then this handsome man gets out, walks around the car and opens the door. Just imagine her surprise when she saw little Vera Adamson get out."

"I can't imagine," said Beth.

"I hear tell he's renting a house from Joe Parker. Joe says he pays cash every month, that he takes him to be a millionaire who has houses all over the world. What do you think's keeping him here?"

"I don't know. Business, maybe."

"Maybe. Or maybe it's our little Vera."

Mrs. Adamson bowed her head and began lightly raking the yard. She could barely hide the smile of parental pride that brightened her face.

Chapter Four

VERA AND RAFE had become an item. They went everywhere together. It seemed as if they enjoyed so many of the same things: outdoor walks, cooking special meals, perceiving everything as an occasion to celebrate.

It was now early autumn, and it seemed as if the world radiated their love; the turning leaves, the occasional cool breeze, indeed everything seemed to echo their anticipation, the elusive beauty of a transitory season. Even songs on the radio seemed to take on a certain meaning to Vera.

It was after several weeks of seeing only each other that the smooth veneer of their relationship received its first chink.

Vera was to accompany Rafe to the Rotary Club dinner dance. When he arrived at her home to pick her up, Vera opened the door to greet him, and his face fell.

"Is this a joke?" he asked.

"What do you mean?"

"I didn't realize it was Halloween."

"Rafe, what are you talking about?"

"What you're wearing—you look ridiculous," he said coldly.

Vera looked at her clothes, which she had bought just for this occasion. She was wearing black satin pants and a sequined sweater; an outfit she considered appropriate for a dinner dance. "What do you mean, Rafe?"

"What? Are you trying to embarrass me? Come on, Vera. Be a good girl and go change into something else. How about that black sweater dress you look so great in? Hurry up, we don't have much time."

Vera walked obediently into her bedroom, fighting back tears and a handful of emotions. She thought she had looked stylish, pretty, maybe even sexy. How could he make such cruel remarks? Well, she'd show him; she just wouldn't go to the stupid dinner dance. Her thoughts drifted. Although then she'd have to face a round of questioning from her parents, who would also be in attendance and would notice her absence, not to mention everyone else in town who kept reminding her what a great catch Rafe was and how lucky she should feel to have snagged him.

"The truth is," Vera thought to herself as she pulled off her clothes, "I usually do feel fortunate to be by Rafe's side. . . and I have been looking forward to being in his arms on the dance floor," she considered as she searched for a pair of black pantyhose that didn't have a run. As she pulled the sweater dress that Rafe had requested over her head, she envisioned them twirling together elegantly, the envy of everyone else at the party. "Maybe he's just had a bad day," she said to herself as she gave her hair a few quick sweeps with a brush. "I'm sure he's probably feeling badly now, and will be a perfect gentleman all evening; we'll have a lovely time together," she said enthusiastically as she gave herself one last spritz of perfume and resolve.

Rafe greeted her with an appreciative smile as he took her arm and wordlessly walked her to the car.

When several weeks passed without another slip-up, Vera was glad she had excused his bad behavior; in fact, he seemed kind, interested, and genuinely supportive of everything she did. Vera considered herself wise to dismiss his previous negative reaction to her with a "Nobody's perfect" and "Everyone's entitled to have a bad day" attitude. After all, shouldn't she practice what she preached? The ability to turn the other cheek was the mark of a good Christian.

Chapter Five

DECEMBER WAS COLD and dreary, and events at the church seemed to chill even the heart.

For months, Vera had become accustomed to a vagrant dropping by the church. He usually came in the mornings. He would get a cup of coffee from the kitchen and, in exchange, leave several shiny silver stones behind on the counter. The man was always wearing the same clothes and, judging from his odor, never seemed to bathe. He wore only a light jacket, and Vera worried about him as she saw him walking up and down Central Avenue in the freezing cold, muttering to himself. Sometimes he would sit in Fellowship Hall and drink his coffee, the gibberish he mumbled punctuated only by occasional nonsensical screaming. He was obviously mentally ill, and as a result was rather intimidating. The church staff left him alone with his coffee.

One day, as Vera made her way to the secretary's office in order to use the copy machine, she was approached by the church's business manager.

"Vera, don't be alarmed by the ambulance in front of the church," the business manager said.

"What? What's happened? Who needs an ambulance?"

"It's just that madman who occasionally stops by for coffee. He collapsed in front of the church."

"What happened? Is he all right?" Vera asked.

"No, I'm not even sure he's still alive. He apparently had some sort of a seizure—the paramedics think he may have had a brain aneurysm. They're taking him to the hospital now to see what can be done."

"Is there any family we can call?" Vera asked.

"No one seems to know."

Vera hesitated, and then asked, "Do we even know his name?"

The business manager shook his head as an answer.

Vera trudged up the stairs to her office, numbed by the news. Vera had seen the man in the church on many occasions, and yet had never spoken to him. She had refrained from breathing through her nose when she needed to pass by him, to escape his foul odor. Truth be told, she had been afraid of the man, or at least of what he represented.

Vera sat behind her desk, thinking of the nameless man who lay dying in some hospital bed, and even in death, as in his life, no one seemed to care. There was no one to hold his hand or say a prayer for him. Vera paused and said a prayer, first asking forgiveness for her own callous attitude toward this poor man, and then asking that his health, mental, emotional, and physical, be returned to him if it be God's will.

She called the hospital to inquire about his condition and learned that he had died in the emergency room shortly after his arrival.

Vera sat at her desk, feeling stunned. She hoped that the man had a loved one to greet him on the other side, and that possibly, through death, his life might become more beautiful and complete.

"Are you okay?" Rafe asked Vera at dinner that evening. "You seem sad."

"I guess I'm all right. I'm just feeling a little blue as a result of something that happened at the church today." Vera recounted the incident to him.

"I keep thinking about all the beautiful funeral and memorial services I've attended in our church," Vera continued. "Last month we had a United States senator serve as a pallbearer, and a couple of months before that, our state governor, a presidential hopeful, was here for the same reason. There was lots of publicity and fanfare when these distinguished men visited, but no one, myself included—no, me especially—ever really paid attention to a man in need who fell down, dying, right in front of our church steps."

Vera sniffled and then continued, "I'm as guilty as anyone, Rafe. Sometimes it seems as if the church becomes so consumed with maintaining its own building, staff, and membership that we forget our primary purpose. It's like we get so absorbed with admiring our own stained glass windows that we forget to look out them and witness a world that is hurting and hungry for our compassion and care."

She started crying, and Rafe took her in his arms. "No one even knew his name, Rafe," she said through her tears. "And it's almost Christmas."

Later, after she had regained her composure, Vera asked Rafe about his own family. "Didn't you first say that you came to Mountain Ridge in order to find out more about your birth parents?"

"Yes."

"And have you?"

"Yes. I know who I am now. But that's no longer the reason I'm here," he said, gently stroking her hair. "I'm here because of you."

Chapter Six

THE CHRISTMAS SEASON continued; for Vera, the contrast between the festivity and human heartache continued as well.

She was serving lunch one day at the local Crisis Intervention Center when she noticed a little boy, about age four, hanging onto his mother's leg.

"Merry Christmas," she greeted him cheerily, handing his mother their soup and sandwiches. She bent down to his level. "I bet you're all ready for Christmas. Have you picked out what you'd like Santa to bring you?"

"Santa may not make it to our house this year," his mother said stiffly.

Vera straightened and looked at her inquisitively.

"I took a job on the night shift so I could spend more time with my older kids, helping them with homework and stuff. I got laid off a couple of months ago—the company closed their nighttime manufacturing division."

"I'm so sorry," Vera said.

"Well, that was bad enough, but then my husband lost his job."

"You're kidding? Both of you?" Vera asked.

"Yes'm. We've had a real tough time tryin' to keep up with our bills. Nearly lost our car and our trailer. My husband got hired somewhere else a couple of weeks ago, but we're so far behind now, we can't afford to buy any gifts for Christmas."

"Let me see what I can do to help you," Vera responded. "If you give me the names and ages and Christmas gift wish lists of your kids I can distribute this information to members of my church who like to lend a helping hand to people in need, especially this time of year. I'll collect some toys for the children and have our Witness Committee get a food basket together for your family. I can also introduce you to someone who can evaluate you and determine what other types of financial assistance you may qualify to receive."

The mother and child followed Vera into the next room. "I sure appreciate this," the woman said with tears in her eyes. "I've never had such bad luck. I was wondering what I was going to do—" she looked cautiously at her youngest child and whispered to Vera, "my kids still believe in Santa."

Early in the evening on December twenty-third, Vera received two phone calls. Both of them were disturbing.

The first phone call was from a long-time friend. Nan had moved from Mountain Ridge years ago when she married an air force pilot, but the former college roommates had always remained close, despite the distance that separated them.

"Vera? Hi, it's Nan. I just wanted to wish you a Merry Christmas."

"Nan! I was going to call you tomorrow for the same reason. Merry Christmas! How are you?"

Vera heard sobbing. "Nan, are you okay? What's wrong?"

"I'm sorry. I thought I could get through this. I didn't know who else to call."

"I'm glad you called me. Now tell me what's the matter. Is it Chris? Are the kids all right?"

Vera heard crying again. "It's Chris. They've called him overseas. He's stationed somewhere in the Balkans; they won't even tell me where, and he'll be there at least until March."

"Oh, Nan! I'm so sorry."

"Me, too. I'm really worried about him. There's so much fighting going on over there. What if we never see him again?"

"I'm sure he'll be all right," Vera said, trying to comfort her friend. "How are the kids holding up?"

"They seem okay. They want their daddy to be home for Christmas," she said, her voice breaking. "I told them we'll have another Christmas when daddy comes home, that they're lucky that they get two Christmases. They seemed to like that idea. It's kinda hard on me, though, trying to always act like everything's all right."

Vera admired her friend's display of strength and courage, while recognizing that Nan had no other choice than to be strong for her children, who needed her and depended on her for love and comfort and guidance.

"Listen, I need to look at my calendar and rearrange my schedule. I'll call you tomorrow and let you know when I can come up for a visit."

"Thanks, Vera. That would help a lot."

"And Nan? I'll keep you in my prayers."

Her friend sniffled. "Thanks. You don't know how much that means to me, especially now."

"I love you and I'll talk to you tomorrow."

The second call was even more disturbing. It was from her minister, notifying Vera that one of the youngest members of their congregation, Ashley, was on life support at Children's Hospital and wasn't expected to live. The suspected cause of the injuries was child abuse.

That night, Vera and Rafe had dinner at her parents' home. Her grandmother joined them for a pre-Christmas Eve feast, as it would be less hectic than revolving around the church worship schedule and gift-wrapping plans of the following day.

As they gathered around the table, Vera's father asked her if she would say the blessing.

Vera bowed her head. "Creator God, thank you for this lovely meal, for the gift of family and the opportunity for us to gather together and count our many blessings. We take time to remember those who are less fortunate, and are reminded that 'shit happens' in this world. But as a result of the greatest of gifts, which we celebrate as the birth of Christ, we can find a sense of peace during times of turmoil, grace among the ugliness, and God's light in the midst of apparent darkness. We thank you for your love and ask for your guidance so that we may reflect your love to others. Amen."

As Vera and Rafe served themselves a buffet supper from the sideboard, they talked together quietly.

"That was some prayer, Vera. Are you drunk?"

"You know I've only had one glass of wine, Rafe. Why, do I seem drunk?"

"Well, I've never heard anyone say 'shit happens' during a prayer before. Especially at a family dinner at Christmas time."

Vera returned the serving spoon back to the bowl of mashed potatoes and sighed. "I know. I guess it was a little outrageous, but I meant it. Shit does happen in this world: ugly, hurtful things that are beyond our control or understanding. I've just seen so much of it lately and I can't seem to get it off my mind. It's like I'm hurting along with these people. The pain, the suffering, the loneliness, the lack of a sense of peace—it seems incongruous with religion, or a sense of God's love, especially at this time of year when we celebrate the birth of the Prince of Peace."

Rafe nodded his head. "But we all go through pain or misfortune in our lives, Vera. None of us are immune to it."

"I know. You can't escape it. I think that's where God fits in. His love is a comfort during inevitable times of grief and despair."

"But the question is, does he cause these feelings of grief and despair?"

"What do you mean, Rafe?" Vera asked.

"I mean, you call God 'the Creator of the universe,' right?"

"Right," Vera answered.

"Then wouldn't it follow that he is responsible for these feelings of pain?"

"I don't know," Vera answered hesitantly.

"Or could it be, perhaps, some evil force that causes these painful situations?"

"I suppose so." Vera took her plate and began moving slowly toward the table.

Rafe followed her. "But the Bible says that your God is the most powerful."

Vera looked at Rafe. "He is the only God."

"But you do acknowledge a conflict between forces of good and evil?"

"Yes, there are many scriptural references to the conflict between good and evil, which I think that anyone living in this world today can attest to. Everyone has experienced the power of temptation."

"But you consider your understanding of God, this God of goodness, to be more powerful."

"Yes," Vera stated firmly. "He is omnipotent."

Rafe followed her. "So, your omnipotent, all-powerful God, in that respect, would have to at least allow these bad things to happen."

Vera set her plate down at the table and turned toward Rafe. "Possibly. We know that this earthly life is filled with conflict and turmoil and temptation."

Rafe wrinkled his brow. "Right. And we know that resulted from Adam and Eve eating the forbidden fruit in the Garden of Eden."

"Yes," Vera answered, assuming the tone of a church professional. "That's the Biblical story that simplistically puts forth the idea of man's original sin, and the freedom of choice, along with all its consequences, that was given to humans as a result."

Rafe took a sip of wine. "So, in that context this world might be a huge playing field, and in this earthly life we must continually make choices between right and wrong that will ultimately affect the score, the ultimate outcome, of this conflict between good and evil in which we are mere players?"

Vera smiled. "That's an interesting way of looking at it. The truth is, we don't know, and possibly can't know during this lifetime. That's where faith comes in. But questioning, and gaining insights from others, can place us farther along the road of our personal faith journey."

"So you don't mind my playing 'devil's advocate' with you?" Rafe asked, raising his eyebrow while smiling at her boyishly.

"Not at all," Vera beamed back at him. "As a matter of fact, I've grown to enjoy it."

They were interrupted by the loud noise of Vera's father clearing his throat, signaling them to attention. He raised his glass officiously. "I'd like to propose a toast."

Earlier, the older adults had left Rafe and Vera alone, since they were so quietly absorbed in their own conversation.

"Vera's beau certainly seems to be taken with her," Vera's grandmother remarked to her son-in-law, "even after that odd prayer of hers."

Vera's father flinched. It was true that Vera had never been typical, had never followed any sort of guidelines imposed by society. Truth was that he had given up hope of Vera ever settling down with anyone, for what man would accept her untamable spirit? Vera's father knew that strong or even rebellious qualities could be considered by men to be attractive traits, but that was with wild girls, and his Vera wasn't wild. Untamable, yes, but wild?

No. For even though she couldn't be swayed by society's expectations, she strictly adhered to those of her true father, God. Vera's one loyalty was to her Creator. She was loving and loyal to people only through the guidelines and standards that trickled down as a result of her devotion to her Redeemer. Vera's dad's heart ached when he considered the seemingly lonely life she had chosen, although he had always been proud of her strong and resolute spirit. But now, as he observed Vera and Rafe deep in conversation, he felt hopeful. Had Vera finally met her match?

"That Rafe certainly is a looker," Vera's grandmother remarked to her daughter. "He must be pretty serious about Vera if he gave up spending time with his own family during the holidays so that he could be with her."

"Actually, Mother, I don't think that Rafe has much family."

"No family? What are you talking about, Beth?"

"Well, Vera tells me that Rafe was adopted at birth, and his adoptive parents were killed in a car accident a couple of years ago. I believe that trying to get more information about his birth parents is what originally brought him to Mountain Ridge."

"Did he find out anything?"

"Not that I know of. Evidently it's a little bit of a sore subject with him."

"And that was months ago, right?"

"Yes, late this past summer."

"So what's keeping him here now?"

Vera's mother and grandmother glanced at Vera as she spoke so intensely with Rafe, and then looked back at each other and smiled.

The two older women carried the rolls and butter to the table. "So what does he do, anyway?" Vera's grandmother asked Beth.

"Evidently, he travels quite a bit. Vera says he's in sales of some sort, but it doesn't look like he works too hard to me. He must have received quite a sizable inheritance from his adoptive parents' estate."

The two women took their places on either side of Vera's father, who sat at the head of the table.

As if on cue, Mr. Adamson raised his glass as he proposed a toast: "To good food, good family, and good friends," he said, gesturing toward Rafe. "I am accustomed to finding myself surrounded by beautiful women, but Rafe, you are a welcome addition to our family. We're glad you could join us."

They clinked their glasses and drank the red wine, completely absorbed by the beauty and merriment of the moment.

Chapter Seven

JANUARY IS THE bleakest month. The holiday gaiety has ended, and the winter seems endless. All the world seems dead, barren, and utterly final. The cold is unrelenting, keeping all color and warmth prisoner.

Rafe and Vera walked the desolate street near his home one Saturday afternoon in January. By walking, they hoped to inject some vitality into their own bodies, since the rest of the world seemed to be completely void of energy.

It was the first time they had seen each other since Vera had gone to visit her friend, Nan.

"So how was your friend?" Rafe asked Vera as they walked.

"Nan? She's fine; as well as could be expected. She puts up a brave front for the kids, but she's worried sick about her husband's safety."

"I guess she doesn't have many other options," Rafe remarked.

"Hmmm?" Vera kicked an icy rock out of the road. "What do you mean?"

"I mean, all she can do is be brave and hope for the best."

"Well, actually, she does have other options, but Nan's strong spirit wouldn't allow her to take them," Vera remarked.

"Like what?"

"Like, she could become hopeless. She could become a blubbering idiot. She could lean on her young children for support. She could blame God."

"I guess blaming God could be a natural response."

"Let's not get into that again!" Vera laughed. "I think I preached that lesson to you before Christmas!"

Rafe laughed and raised his hands in the air as if to surrender.

"But seriously—"

"Ha!, I knew you couldn't help but elaborate! See, you weren't quite finished preaching to me after all!" Rafe teased.

Vera punched him in the arm good-naturedly. "No, Rafe, really. This is important. I know we talked about why crisis or conflict might occur in our lives, but we didn't talk about how people deal with it."

"Go on, I'm listening." Rafe dug his hands in his pockets.

"Well, when misfortune occurs, and we agreed that it does occur in every person's life—"

"Right, go on."

"Well, you know how you hypothesized that our earthly lives might be part of some eternal testing ground?"

"You mean that we're constantly tested, and how we react to these tests may affect the ultimate outcome of this cosmic game in which we all play?"

"Exactly. Well, if that's the case, then how we react to conflict or misfortune would be of supreme importance," Vera added.

"How so?" Rafe asked.

"Well, it seems to me that when a person is 'tested,' as you say, he or she can respond in a variety of different ways . . . well, two actually."

Rafe smiled, "Please enlighten me."

"Simply speaking, a person can use this conflict or misfortune in one of two ways: to make him or her become either stronger or weaker."

"Stronger or weaker? How?"

"Well," Vera continued, "If you surrender to the test—if you let misfortune beat you—then you become weaker. You've given in; you've let the conflict win and take over your life mentally, physically, emotionally, and spiritually."

"I think I know what you mean," Rafe interjected. "I've actually met people who let the crisis become their life. It's like they wear this name badge that says, 'Hello, my name is so-and-so, and I'm the way I am because . . .' The blanks are filled in with different names and excuses, such as, 'I lost my job,' 'my child died,' and 'my health failed,' but the response they expect always seems to be the same: 'feel sorry for me because I am a victim of a cruel fate.'"

"That may be a little harsh, Rafe. Fate can be cruel, and we shouldn't judge unless we've experienced the same pain."

They walked a little ways wordlessly.

Vera interrupted their silent thoughts: "My experience from working with others at the church who have suffered misfortune has led me to believe that pain, misfortune, difficulty, tragedy, loss . . . however you experience it, is like a fire."

Rafe turned toward her, his interest piqued.

"A fire . . . how so?" he asked.

Vera shuffled on, trying to frame her thoughts. "Well, misfortune is like a fire, a huge fire that enters and begins to absorb your life . . ."

Rafe was obviously fascinated. "Yes . . . go on," he prompted.

"It's like . . . if you try to avoid the flames, the fire will consume you, your life." Vera continued walking, trying to give words to her impressions. "It's like you have to embrace the flames, meet them head-on, in order to extinguish them."

"Ouch," Rafe grimaced comically, "that sounds painful."

"It is. Very." Vera said, her brow still furrowed in thought. She then chuckled, her wrinkles erasing.

"What?" Rafe smiled, grabbing her hand.

"I was just reminded of a saying of my father's . . . handed down from my father's college track coach, actually." Vera said, smiling to herself.

"Well, what is it?" Rafe coaxed, swinging her hand. "Tell me."

"As my father tells it, the track and field team would be in training, and evidently this coach would really push them to their limit, making them run past the point of exhaustion, until they felt as if they were either about to faint or throw their guts up, and then he'd say to them: 'it takes fire to temper steel'."

"Interesting. Were they a winning team?" Rafe asked.

Vera nodded her head yes.

Rafe walked beside Vera silently, digesting this thought.

After a while, Rafe responded, "So that's the second option . . . facing the fire?"

"Yes, the most difficult one. It's where you look pain in the eye and say, 'I can handle this. I will survive this. I will use this misfortune to make me a stronger and better person.'"

"Wow. That is tough. Doesn't that sort of belligerence toward pain harden a person?" Rafe asked.

"It can, yes. But with the guidance of God, as well as the help of the Holy Spirit who fortifies us with courage and peace, we can become better, stronger people."

"New and improved, huh?" Rafe joked. "So next time I land on 'misfortune,' in this Monopoly game of life, I should use bravery rather than self-pity in order to 'get out of jail.'"

"Whatever you think, Rafe," Vera said, smiling faintly. As they began climbing the incline of a steep hill, they trudged upwards in silence.

After the hill, they reached a level road and regained their breath.

"Man, the whole world looks dead from up here," Rafe remarked, looking at the valley laid out beneath them. "It's almost as if we're the lone survivors of a nuclear holocaust or something."

Rafe's remark reflected Vera's own thoughts. A few tendrils of smoke emanating from chimneys were the only evidence of life or movement. The dead grass was sheathed in ice; the dark tree branches were bare. There were no songbirds, no squirrels, no flowers, no noise. It seemed as if life had stopped, frozen for eternity. They stood together in silence.

"How do you find the love and energy of the Creator in this, Vera?" Rafe knew how Vera spiritually recharged her batteries off the beauty of the earth.

Vera continued staring. "It's hard. Even I feel numb. It's hard to remember what this landscape looks like when colored with the lushness of life. It's a lesson in faith."

"It's amazing how you find some sort of spiritual lesson in everything you encounter," Rafe teased. "Okay, I'll give. How is this a lesson in faith?"

Vera ignored his comments as her gloved hand stroked a tree branch that was hanging low beside the road. "What does this tree branch look like to you?"

"I don't know. It looks dead."

"Exactly. And what do you think it will look like in four or five months?"

"Duh, that's a toughie," Rafe said mockingly. "It will be covered in leaves, of course."

"Right, and this particular tree is a dogwood, so it will even be filled with flowers, like a colorful bouquet."

"So?"

"So right now it's hard to imagine this bare, dead-looking branch in full bloom. That's what faith is: believing in something that doesn't seem apparent; putting trust that beauty will abound in its own time."

Rafe chuckled, "Vera, some people consider a bare frozen branch to be beautiful in itself. You really don't like winter, do you?"

Vera looked embarrassed. "It's okay . . . I mean it's not my favorite season. I guess I like it as a transition. I wouldn't appreciate spring so much if winter didn't seem to become so long and dreary. It does seem as if my heart saddens each year with the killing frost."

"The 'killing frost'?" Rafe asked.

"That's what people around here call the first frost of autumn that kills anything tender that may still be growing."

"Anything tender?"

"You know, summertime flowers, vegetables still growing in the garden . . . that sort of thing."

"Oh. The 'killing frost' . . . Another quaint colloquialism I'll have to add to my new vocabulary list, along with the 'Deer Woods.'"

Vera laughed. "So you've heard of the Deer Woods, eh? You must be becoming one of us after all!"

"You laugh, but did you know that after Joe, my landlord, mentioned that he was going to the Deer Woods, I actually got out an area map and tried to locate them?"

"You didn't!" Vera squealed with laughter.

"It wasn't until Betty MacPherson, at the grocery store, explained to me that people use that expression for any woods during the deer hunting season, that I knew what everyone was talking about, or where all the men had gone. You let me down, Vera. I rely on you to be my interpreter for this sort of thing."

"I guess I just take it for granted that things like that are universal knowledge." She stopped walking and bowed dramatically in a prostrate position. "I do humbly beg your forgiveness, kind sir. It will never happen again."

He laughed and pulled her close to him. "Well, see that it doesn't. I depend on you to make me look good," he teasingly chastised her.

They walked along together for a while, breathing in the cool winter air.

Rafe broke the silence.

"So your idea of hell would be an eternal icy tundra?"

Rafe's voice startled Vera from her thoughts. "Huh? Oh," she laughed, catching onto his line of thought. "Yeah, probably," she admitted.

Vera continued to look around her at the icy picture laid out before her. After a while, she continued, "The starkness of this frozen landscape does have a certain beauty, a severe crystalline contrast between dark and light. There's a hidden energy in this landscape, a promise of potential. It reminds me of a poem, a sonnet, actually, written in the seventeenth century by John Donne. It's called 'Batter My Heart, Three-Personed God.'"

"Here we go again," Rafe laughed. "'Batter My' what?"

"'Batter My Heart, Three-Personed God,'" Vera continued, ignoring his teasing. "It's a poem in which Donne compares his heart, his soul, his love of God to a prisoner held captive behind fortress walls. He asks God to 'break, blow, burn and make me new.' He goes on to say that his heart is held captive and 'proves weak or untrue,' and that he would love God if he were not 'betroth'd unto your enemie.' Then, in the last quatrain, he asks that God

> "*Divorce mee, untie, or breake that knot againe,*
> *Take mee to you, imprison mee, for I,*
> *Except you enthrall mee, never shall be free,*
> *Nor ever chaste, except you ravish mee."*

"Wow, I'm impressed," Rafe commented.

Vera blushed. "Well, you know us English majors."

"But what does it mean? Could you explain it to me?" Rafe asked.

"Well, it means that his heart has become frozen, like what we're seeing now. He is numb to God's love as a result of being taken prisoner, or becoming betrothed to evil. The sonnet asks God to break down the fortress walls surrounding his heart and rescue or reclaim him, and in the last startling lines he says that he will only become pure or chaste by being raped, or ravished, by God."

"Wow. So getting fucked by God is a good thing," Rafe commented.

Vera looked at him, and then looked away. "I guess it's a matter of perspective," she said as she began walking down the hill.

Vera met her friend Maggy for dinner and a movie that night.

"Hey girl! How are you?" Maggy said as they met and quickly hugged before walking into the restaurant. "I can't believe we even live in the same town. I never see you anymore."

The two were seated at a booth. "I guess I've been kind of busy," Vera confessed. "I'm sorry if I haven't been a very good friend lately."

"Busy?" Maggy shrieked. "Don't give me that load of crap. You forget who you're talking to. I know where you've been spending your time, or I should say with whom you've been spending your time. Wake up, Vera, the whole town's talking about you and Rafe, and I want to hear all the details."

Vera smiled. She had missed her friend's directness. "I don't know. What do you think?"

"Think? Who needs to think? All I would be able to do is feel if I spent any amount of time around that handsome hunk of yours. And I bet I'd be feelin' pretty good."

Vera laughed and picked up a menu. "He is kind of cute, isn't he?"

"Kind of cute? That's the understatement of the year. Cute is what you call a kitten, Vera, not someone as . . . as indescribably gorgeous as Rafe. Now have mercy on your deadbeat married friend and give me some details before I go crazy!"

Vera laughed again, enjoying her friend's company. They ordered their dinner, and as the waitress walked away from their table, Maggy began again.

"Okay, girlfriend. Spill it!"

"Maggy, you're relentless!"

Maggy gave her an undaunted stare.

"Okay, okay. There's not much to tell, really. Rafe and I have just been enjoying each other's company. We walk, we talk a lot, we go out to eat—"

"You two sound like a couple of Barbie dolls. Excuse me, I stand corrected. You're more like Ken and Barbie."

Vera giggled. She had never been part of a couple before, and she was enjoying the attention, the status it seemed to have given her.

"So, what's he like?" Maggy asked as she slurped up her soup.

"He's hard to get to know, actually."

"Reserved, huh?"

"Yes, that's it exactly." Vera said.

"Man, those reserved types can drive you crazy. It's like you become obsessed with them letting you in. You better be careful, girlfriend. Don't drop your guard."

"What do you mean?" Vera said, taking a bite out of her sandwich.

"I mean, don't give him all the power."

"You're not making any sense, Maggy, talking about dropping my guard and giving him power. I'm talking about a relationship here. You sound as if Rafe is some enemy spy."

"Listen, Vera, you're inexperienced in relationships. I just don't want you to get hurt. If Rafe hangs back and won't invest himself emotionally, then you need to be careful. I know you. You love everyone, and if you make yourself vulnerable to Rafe while he remains distant or aloof, then he might stomp all over that big beautiful heart of yours."

"It's not that way, Maggy. Rafe is very kind and caring." Vera played with her potato chips. "I just think that he didn't have a very secure childhood, and it's difficult for him to express his feelings."

"Okay, okay, I've said my piece," Maggy said, raising her hands in mock surrender.

"He really is a very nice person. He's so interested in everything I do." Vera was still defending Rafe.

"Yeah, yeah, so he's nice." Maggy moved her face closer to Vera's. "What I really want to know is if he's a good kisser."

Vera blushed.

"Well, I can see by the look on your face that he is. Have you two gone all the way yet?"

"Maggy!"

"What? You can't blame a girl for asking!"

"Of course we haven't gone all the way!"

"Wake up, Vera. You're the only twenty-five-year-old virgin in the country."

"You don't have to act like I'm some kind of freak."

"I'm sorry," Maggy apologized. "I was out of line. It's just . . . Rafe's a grown man. Don't you think that after a while he's going to, you know, expect something to happen?"

"Actually, between his traveling and my crazy work schedule, we don't get to see each other very often." Vera etched the tablecloth with the back of her fork. "Rafe knows how I feel. How special I want it to be," she said quietly.

"And?"

"And he's been very patient. I think he thinks that I'm special, that it's something worth waiting for," Vera said.

"What, exactly, if you don't mind my asking, are you waiting for?" Maggy asked.

"It's hard to explain, really. The right person, the right time, the right situation. I want to know that I love and am loved by this person, and that he treasures me, and my virginity, as a gift. It's a gift I want to share with only one man, the right man, who I'll love and who will love me for the rest of my life," Vera answered.

"Well good luck, Cinderella. Do you, by chance, think that Rafe might be the right man?"

Vera looked up at her friend. "I think so," she smiled.

The two were quiet for a while.

Vera interrupted the silence. "Maggy, can I ask you something? I mean, you're married and all, maybe you could help me understand."

"Sure, sweetie," Maggy said as she forked a bite full of pie into her mouth. "I'll try. What can I help you with?"

"Well, do guys . . . I mean, you know, when Rafe and I first started going out, he was always so kind, so courteous, so thoughtful—"

"And now?" Maggy helped her friend along.

"Now, sometimes he's a smart ass." She grinned at her friend.

"Well, welcome to couplehood. You two really are in a relationship if he already feels comfortable enough to be a smart ass."

Vera smiled. "No, really, be serious."

"I am being serious. He must feel comfortable with you if he's letting down his guard like that. Vera, let me enlighten you with a truth of nature: all guys are smart asses."

"No, they're not."

"Yes, they are. And the longer you're in a relationship with one of them, the more they'll reveal this to you. Rafe's not different from any other guy if he's occasionally being rude. Consider it a compliment. It means he likes you."

"I'm not any good at this stuff," Vera said, exasperated.

"You'll learn. If rudeness or arrogance are Rafe's only bad qualities, then hang onto him, honey. He's rich; he's handsome; he seems to adore you. You could do a lot worse," Maggy said as she picked up the check and walked toward the register.

Chapter Eight

"WOW!" VERA SAID to Rafe as they walked out the front doors of the church on Sunday morning. "Wasn't that a great service?"

"I don't know about 'great,'" Rafe responded.

"Well, it was just what I needed. I feel exhilarated. The music, the scripture, everything seemed to speak to me."

"I thought you thought of church as an antiquated institution," Rafe said as they walked toward his car.

"I do think that certain components are outdated, or not in touch with people's needs today, but for the life of me I can't think of a better way to worship."

"How about by yourself?" Rafe asked as he opened her car door.

"Well, as individuals we should always be prayerful and meditate about God's meaning in our lives and for our lives," she said to him as he slid into the seat next to her, "but sometimes I think we need to meet as a group in order to receive inspiration."

"You mean that 'Where two or more are gathered in my name' thing?"

"Exactly. Honestly, I've given it a lot of thought and I can't think of a better way to worship corporately than in a church setting."

"But doesn't a lot of the spirituality get lost in the bureaucracy?" Rafe asked.

"Yes, some does. But I've seen churches that have broken away from their denomination in order to get away from that structured order and, ironically, as the church grows and their memory fades, they recreate the church as an organization. I guess it's a necessary evil."

"Hmmm," said Rafe as he drove toward the restaurant.

After they placed their lunch order, Vera tucked her menu back behind the box of napkins on their table. "I've really got to stop eating like this. I've been going out to eat so much lately, and at Youth Group meetings I always eat pizza or nachos or hot dogs with the kids. Last Lock-In we had fun pigging out on doughnuts."

"I guess that explains your fat ass," Rafe remarked while looking at his menu. He then folded the menu and placed it on the table with his hands folded on top of it. He looked at her, smugly smiling.

Vera looked at him, shocked. She could tell by his demeanor that he hadn't been teasing her. Did he really think that she was fat, or had he only meant to hurt her feelings? Vera couldn't tell.

Vera felt as if someone had knocked the breath out of her. She couldn't think of anything to say.

Rafe stared at her blankly across the table. He obviously didn't feel as if he had said anything wrong.

Vera wanted to cry. She was hurt and felt self-conscious that this man she loved obviously considered her to be fat. Quietly she picked at her food, waiting for the meal to mercifully end so that she could return home.

Midway through the meal, Rafe started a conversation as if nothing had happened.

"So what do you think the minister meant in his sermon when he said that many religions worship different versions of the same God?" Rafe asked.

Vera didn't look up. "He meant that many religions such as Buddhism, Hinduism, Islam, and others are different cultural translations of the same God, the one God."

"But aren't the teachings of Buddha, Mohammed, and Christ different?"

"They're different, but similar. They each point to eternal truths."

"Eternal truths? Like what?"

"Listen, Rafe, I've really got a lot of work to do at home and need to be getting back. If you'd like I can give you some books to read and you can discover these truths for yourself."

"I'm almost done, and then I'll get the check," he said as he cleaned the remaining food off his plate.

Days passed before Rafe and Vera spoke again. Vera threw herself into her work at the church and was simply unavailable. Toward the end of the week, Rafe finally got through to her on her office phone.

"Vera? Hi stranger. I've missed you. How have you been?"

"Busy," Vera replied coldly as she stood and pulled the long phone cord taut.

"I can tell. You must be living at the church these days."

Vera paused and twisted the phone cord around her index finger. She really didn't want to talk to him, and yet she didn't want to be rude. "Just about. I really don't have time to talk now; you just caught me on my way to a Worship Committee meeting."

"Another meeting? How many committees do you have down there anyway?"

Vera smiled faintly and began pacing the two steps backward and forward that the phone cord would allow. "Countless, it seems. There's a lot to be done to plan for Lent."

"Lent? Wow, I guess spring is really creeping up on me this year. I can't believe it's nearly Easter."

"Well, it's nearly the Lenten season anyway, the period in which we prepare ourselves for Easter."

Rafe chuckled, "And so your job is to prepare for the preparation?"

Vera laughed, "I guess so."

"Well, I won't keep you, then. I just wanted to let you know that I've been called out of town. There's a sales seminar I need to attend, and I'll be away for several days."

"Oh."

"I'll be thinking of you while I'm gone, Vera."

Vera sat down in her desk chair again. "Okay, Rafe. Thanks for calling."

"Bye," he said softly.

"Bye," she responded likewise.

Vera quietly hung up the phone, leaving her hand on the receiver for some minutes as she stared into space and thought of nothing at all.

Chapter Nine

VERA ENJOYED THE first days of Rafe's absence. She shared time with her friends and parents, catching up quietly with the people she loved. The weather was getting warmer outside, and Vera felt warmer inside, too, as she nurtured her inner self in preparation for the spiritual season of spring.

Everything seemed so easy. There were no schedules to keep, no required conversational responses, and no meals to prepare, or even eat for that matter.

Vera took long walks. She enjoyed feeling her blood stir and felt in harmony with the trees around her, whose sluggish sap also stirred in an effort to put forth leaves.

Nothing was required of her. Life seemed carefree and easy. As she walked, Vera's soul sang a loud song of love and happiness and peace and thanksgiving for the world around her.

Even as she drove her car, Vera said silent prayers for every person she passed.

Vera did not have to justify being alone, for most of the town seemed to know that Rafe was away on business. Her neighbors and co-workers seemed to take special care to smile at Vera as if to say, "We know you're alone," "We hope you're not lonely," or even "We've missed our girl."

But then the days passed into weeks, with still no word from Rafe.

Truth be told, Vera had initially been thankful for Rafe's absence. Her feelings had been hurt and she needed time to mend, to reevaluate, to understand the meaning he had in her life.

At first, she had barely missed him, she had so enjoyed nurturing and celebrating her life as an individual.

But as the days passed, Vera became more confused. She wondered if he had tired of her, and simply moved on to a life without her.

Vera read similar questions in the eyes of others that asked, "Is Rafe back yet?" or "Have you heard from Rafe?" or "When's that man of yours coming home?" Vera wished she had an answer for them. As the townspeople's questions subsided, Vera knew that even they were giving up hope and beginning to pity Vera, who seemed to have been abandoned.

Rafe's absence had caused her to question her feelings for him. She knew now that she loved him. She loved him as she had loved no other man. She had given him her heart, and now she would never be the same. In her mind she replayed the many times they had shared together, asking herself what she had done wrong, how she could have proven herself more worthy of his companionship.

It was true that he had hurt her feelings a few times, but Vera knew she was a sensitive person, which enabled her to be more caring and giving toward others, but also made her more vulnerable to being hurt. Perhaps she had been too sensitive or expected too much. Vera knew from witnessing her own parents' relationship that maintaining love requires a constant give-and-take synchronization; maybe she had only placed herself on the receiving end, and hadn't given Rafe the time and energy necessary to understand and fulfill his own needs.

Vera wasn't sure of anything anymore. She had never felt so alone.

After nearly a month's absence, Vera finally heard from Rafe. "Vera? Hi, sweetheart, it's Rafe."

"Rafe?"

"Man, it's good to hear your voice. I can hardly wait to see you again."

"Rafe, where are you?" Vera asked.

"I'm on way back to Mountain Ridge now. Listen, honey, I'm sorry I've been gone so long, but I've been sent on one assignment after another. Headquarters has really kept me hopping, and I've been traveling from one place to another with hardly a moment's rest."

"When will you be back?" Vera asked.

"I should be back late tonight. How about if I pick you up at your place late tomorrow afternoon, and we spend a quiet evening together?"

"That sounds nice. I'm looking forward to seeing you again," Vera said.

"Me too, baby. They're boarding my flight, so I've got to run. I'll be in touch again soon."

"Okay, Rafe. Good-bye."

"Bye."

Vera hung up the phone and hugged herself. He was coming home. He had missed her. Everything was all right. Vera smiled to herself and reached for the phone to tell her mother the good news.

Vera opened the door the next evening and Rafe scooped her up in his arms. He squeezed her and held her tight, without saying a word, for several minutes. Vera closed her eyes and said a silent prayer of thanks.

He sighed deeply and set her down. "Oh, God, Vera. You don't know how good it is to see you again, to touch you again," he said, sliding the back of his fingers down her cheek and then through her long blonde hair. "I'm sorry, but I've just got to hold you some more," he said as he picked her up and held her in his arms. She squealed with surprise and delight as he hugged her tightly to his chest. "You fit so perfectly in my arms," he said while holding her.

"I think it's where I belong," she said with tears in her eyes. Her cheek was pressed against his and she was inhaling his scent, trying to absorb him into her own system.

He gently pulled away and looked deeply into her eyes while resting his hands on her delicate shoulders.

"My sweet, sweet Vera." Rafe touched the underside of her chin and lifted her face to meet his own. "Will you be mine forever?"

She looked at him for several long moments before answering, "I already am."

They drove to Rafe's house in silence. During the ride, they continuously held hands. They looked at each other and smiled often, occasionally giving the other's hand a squeeze or a light kiss.

Later, upon reflection, Vera would wish that that ride, that journey so filled with love and anticipation, had never ended.

At his home that evening, together they prepared a tossed salad and pasta with red sauce for dinner.

After the meal, they sat in front of the fire that Rafe had prepared in order to take the chill off the evening.

They stared into the flames and sipped their Chianti.

Rafe broke the silence. "Imagining this moment is what got me through the long wintry nights without you, Vera. Right now I feel as if I have everything."

She looked at him. "I know. I don't think I've ever felt so warm, so comfortable, so secure."

"I want it to always be like this, Vera. I want to take care of you, to protect you. I want to be your rock, your source of strength."

It was easy to read her eyes: that was what she wanted, too.

He lowered his face to hers and kissed her passionately.

Vera felt warmth like a wildfire spread from her lips down to her abdomen and legs.

Their bodies, entwined as one, melted into the couch.

Rafe's hand slipped beneath her sweater and cupped her breast. Vera moaned softly as he pushed aside the silky lace of her bra and caressed her hardened nipple.

Their lips were soft and matched each other perfectly as they parted. Their tongues met, softly, tentatively, as they brushed against each other and then pushed harder in urgency. They shared each other's breath and seemingly their souls as they kissed and caressed each other, moving together as one.

Rafe tenderly kissed her nose, her eyes, her cheeks, her neck. Vera gently bit his ear lobe, sucking on the soft flesh. She flicked her tongue into the hidden recesses of his ear and enjoyed hearing him moan in pleasure.

He rose above her, straddling her thighs as she lay on the couch. He began to unbutton her jeans.

"Vera, I want you so much . . . I've waited so long," he said huskily as he pulled at her zipper.

Vera became afraid. "Rafe, wait . . . I'm not sure I'm ready—"

"Oh, you're ready, baby," he said, forcefully stroking the inseam of her jeans, bruising her tender flesh.

"No, really, Rafe," she said, struggling against the weight of his body to get to an upright position.

"Shhhh," he said as he again lowered her body and began kissing her. "I'll take care of you. It will be all right," he said, as if comforting a child.

"No, Rafe. I mean it!" she said, and with a burst of energy she pushed him off of her and stood beside the sofa.

"I just don't think I'm ready yet," she said in defense as she pulled down her sweater. She had enjoyed kissing him, but the recent memory of his unexplained absence made her afraid to completely give in to him.

He stood and moved to the window, his back toward her.

They were quiet for several minutes. The only sound that could be heard was the crackle of the flames consuming the logs in the fireplace.

Vera walked toward him. "Rafe," she said softly as she placed her hand on his shoulder.

He pushed her away violently and spoke in a harsh, measured tone, "Get the hell away from me!"

"But Rafe—"

"I mean it, Vera."

"But I just want to talk."

"Ha! That's an understatement! That's all you ever want to do is . . . talk." He spat the words venomously.

"Rafe, I just—"

"I said get away from me, you bitch. Grow up, Vera, or go play with your God, and your thoughts and ideas about him. Maybe he'll keep you warm at night."

Vera was stunned. She felt as if she were with a stranger. She didn't know what to do and she didn't have a way to leave.

The tears began as extra moisture in her eyes, which she tried to contain. It was important to her to remain strong and to keep her dignity intact. She hadn't done anything wrong, had she?

Maybe she had been wrong, had led him on by kissing him so passionately, she speculated. She had felt so loved and she wanted that wonderful warm feeling to continue. She knew he was a man and had needs to be met, but didn't she have needs, too?

The tears were now streaming down her face. She sank into the nearby club chair and sobbed silently to herself.

Rafe ignored her, continuing to stare out the window.

He began pacing the floor, back and forth in front of the window.

Finally, Vera gained enough composure to utter a few words. "I'd like to go home now, Rafe," she said, trying to keep her voice steady.

"Well, too bad, little girl. You're just going to have to wait. Kinda ironic, huh? Since waiting seems to be an obsession with you." He shoved his hands in his pockets and continued to pace, occasionally socking a sofa cushion or kicking a floor pillow. "Vera," he finally said, "I am so angry, so . . . frustrated right now, that I literally cannot see straight. There's no way I could drive you."

She sat in her chair, still and quiet. She felt badly that she had affected him this way. Finally she said, "Rafe, I'm sorry."

He stopped pacing and leaned against the window. He sighed hugely and said, mostly to the windowpanes, "I'm sorry too, Vera."

She waited a few more minutes before speaking again. "It's just that . . . I don't even know what we have here, Rafe," she said, causing the tears to flow again. "I don't even know who we are . . . together."

He remained motionless, and Vera wasn't sure he had heard her. Finally, he nodded his head as if in agreement, but still he waited before saying, "All I know is that I can't imagine life without you, Vera. I guess I love you."

She studied his silhouette for some time before answering.

"I love you too, Rafe," she said while rising and walking toward him. "I realize now that I've already given you my heart. Maybe I've placed too much value on other things." She took his hands in her own. "All I know, the only thing that's important is that I love you." She still had tears in her eyes. "And as a result of that love, I want to give myself to you: body, mind, and soul."

He lowered his head, resting it against her shoulder. She stroked his hair, comforting him, and then walked with him to his bedroom.

Once they reached his bedroom, they were both shy.

Vera kissed him lightly on the mouth, his cheek, his neck. She unbuttoned the top button of his shirt.

He finished unbuttoning it, and then removed his pants.

Vera pulled her sweater off, and then moved to the bed, removing the pillow shams and pulling the covers down.

She quickly removed her jeans and climbed beneath the covers.

He stood before her. He pulled off his underwear.

Vera wasn't sure what she should do. Should she look at him while he was naked? She didn't want to stare, but it seemed even more awkward to look away.

She looked at him briefly. His chest was dusted with a light frosting of hair that seemed to reach expansively toward his arms and then trail down his belly to his legs.

Vera inhaled quickly as she glanced at his manhood. It seemed as if all the energy, all the masculinity contained in Rafe's body had circulated uncontrollably throughout his body and erupted between his legs.

Vera began busying herself, removing her bra and panties while under the covers and dropping them inconspicuously, she hoped, onto the floor. Rafe climbed in the bed beside her.

When it was over, Vera lay trembling in Rafe's arms.

"This is how it should be," Vera thought to herself. "I am happy. I am with the man I love."

Chapter Ten

A COUPLE OF days later, Vera was sitting at her desk at the church when she heard a familiar singsongy voice. "Knock, knock." Maggy's head peered around the doorway.

"Maggy! How are you? What a nice surprise! Come on in."

Maggy stepped into the office and plopped into a chair in front of Vera's desk.

"I just happened to be downtown shopping and thought I'd pop in and see what my old friend was up to," Maggy said.

"Not too much." Vera gestured at the paperwork on her desk. "Just the usual."

"That's not what I hear," Maggy teased.

"Oh?" Vera looked concerned. "And what do you hear?"

"Well, I've heard that a certain handsome young gentleman has returned to town."

"Rafe?" Vera smiled. "Yeah, he's back."

"How is he?"

Vera smiled at her friend. "Better than ever."

"Oh? Tell me more." Maggy leaned across the desk. "Don't tell me that you two finally . . ."

Vera tried to hide her blush by looking at her folded hands in her lap.

"Why, Miss Vera Adamson! Don't tell me you've been deflowered!"

Vera looked alarmed and whispered loudly, "Would you hush!"

"Sorry, I didn't know it was such a big secret. Well, what was it like?"

"Maggy!"

"Oh come on, it's not like I've never done it before. I was just wondering if it lived up to your expectations."

Vera studied her hands again. "Well, yes and no. I mean, I've never felt closer to Rafe, but I kind of feel like I've lost something, a part of me I can't get back."

Maggy nodded her head in understanding.

"It was probably just the awkwardness of it being the first time for me, but it just didn't feel as . . . comfortable . . . as I expected."

Maggy smiled. "Yeah, I remember my first time, it just didn't seem natural. It felt like someone was trying to push a softball up my nostril or something."

Vera grinned at Maggy. "You're outrageous!"

"I know," she said as she squeezed her friend's hand. "Let's go get some lunch."

Chapter Eleven

LATER THAT AFTERNOON, Vera knocked on Rafe's front door. "Rafe? Sweetheart?" She walked into the kitchen. "I baked some banana bread this afternoon and thought you might like some."

She found him in the den, sealing large boxes with strapping tape.

"What are you up to?" she asked.

"What does it look like? I'm packing."

"Packing? Where are you going?"

"Away."

"Rafe? I don't understand."

"It's simple, Vera. I'm leaving."

"But I thought–"

He straightened and looked at her stonily. "Thought what?"

"The other night . . . we talked about a future together."

"Vera, since you always seem to be searching for the truth, I'm going to give it to you, especially since you can't seem to see it when it's right in front of your eyes." He began packing a box with books. "You know how you're always talking about your God, this Creator, the one true God?"

She nodded her head dumbly.

"Well, you're wrong. He's not the only God. There is another."

"What are you talking about, Rafe? I don't understand."

Rafe slammed a box down to the floor. "Quit being so damn naive, Vera! You think you've got everything figured out. You are so smug, so self-righteous, and yet you're right: you don't understand. You don't understand at all."

"Understand what? Rafe, please help me to sort this out. What's happened to you?"

Rafe took several long strides until he was standing directly in front of her. "Nothing has happened to me, Vera. This is me . . . the real me."

"I don't believe it," Vera said, leaning against a nearby chair for support. "Something's happened to you."

He scoffed, "Yes, you're right. Something has happened to me, for you see, I worship the one, true God, only it's different from the flimsy one you admire. My father is the God of Chaos, from whence we all came, and where we shall all return. We represent the true Alpha, and I am here to see that we are also the Omega, the beginning and the end."

Vera was dazed. "But my God, Yahweh, is the Creator."

Rafe took a step toward her. "Vera, we live in a bipolar, dualistic world. Consider that there is hot and cold, north and south, war and peace, good and evil. The laws of physics state that for every action there is an equal and opposite reaction." He took another half step toward her until he was right in front of her face. "You choose, or are destined, to love and worship God the Creator, but you are wrong to consider him the only God. My father is the God of Destruction. Your concept of what is good and beautiful must be destroyed so that this world can give birth to a different interpretation of beauty."

"What are you talking about? Satan?" Vera asked.

Rafe returned to his boxes. "My father goes by many names," he responded.

"So you're saying that you're Satan's son? Rafe, do you know how stupid that sounds?"

"No more stupid than calling God your father."

Vera leaned forward against a chair. "Let me see if I've got this straight. You're breaking up with me because the Devil made you do it?" she scoffed. "You must really take me for a fool."

Rafe turned quickly, clutched her face tightly in his hand, and stared directly in her eyes as he spoke in a steely tone, "You are correct. I do take you for a fool, but that is beside the point." He released her and she drooped against the chair, stroking her bruised cheeks in disbelief. Rafe continued, "You know, we love that 'devil' thing. It really cracks us up that you all are stupid enough to dismiss the God of Evil as a red cartoon character with a goatee, a pointed tail, and a pitchfork." He paused to look again at Vera. "You all are so much easier to manipulate when you don't consider us a serious threat."

Vera was frightened. Her mind whirled in an effort to understand the situation. "And us? Have you . . . did you deliberately mislead me? You . . . we . . . have always been a lie?" Her voice cracked as she realized that her trust, their declarations of love, and promises of a future together had all been false, a product of Rafe's manipulation.

Rafe walked back to one corner of the room and again began packing boxes. "I was honest when I said I stayed here in Mountain Ridge because of you, because you see, sweetheart, you were my target."

"What?"

"My target. My assignment. You see, Vera, you are a child of light, worshipping God the Creator. You had a unique understanding of the spirituality of the unchurched, knowledge which could have been dangerous to our cause if you had remained on course. My assignment was to get you to share with me."

He began loading another box. "It was a fun project, actually," he said. "I convinced you to give me your heart, your soul . . . ," he looked at her lustily and chuckled, "your body. But most importantly, your understanding of others' spirituality—information that will be most helpful in luring others to the dark side."

Vera tightened her grip on the chair she was leaning against. "This can't be happening to me."

Rafe looked at her contemptuously. "It's time for a reality check, Vera." He began sealing the box he had been packing. "You, in effect, have been neutralized. You are no longer a threat to the dark side." He stacked the box atop another and looked at her. "In fact, now you are nothing. And it's simply time for me to move on."

She caught his gaze and held it. "Rafe, I trusted you."

Rafe stared at her for a moment and then smiled eerily. "Big mistake, babe."

"You bastard!" Vera screamed at him.

Rafe laughed and leaned against a box. "Now you're catching on."

Vera ran out of the house and got in her car, driving away as quickly as possible.

Chapter Twelve

DAYS LATER, RAFE found Vera sitting on a stone wall on top of the mountain where they used to walk.

"Vera?" he called, shining a flashlight in her direction.

She remained silent.

"There you are. I thought you might have come up here. Everybody's worried sick about you; they haven't seen you in days. Your mother called and asked me to look for you."

"That must have given you some satisfaction. You could probably hardly wait to find me, so you could kick me while I'm down. You can leave now, Rafe. You're the big hero now that you've found me. What are you still doing in town anyway?"

"I've . . . been detained."

"Another assignment?" she asked caustically.

"No, it's something more personal. Vera, I think I should get you home. It's dark up here. I don't think it's very safe."

"It is dark up here," she said, looking around. "I can't even see a star in the sky."

"It's overcast. The clouds are covering the starlight," he said.

It began to rain, a constant, cold drizzle.

"Vera, let's go. I'm worried about you."

"It's dark and I can't see anything, Rafe." She was rambling. "I can't even make out what path I should take, much less see my destination." Vera made a sobbing, animalistic noise that almost sounded as if a part of her were breaking. Rafe reached for her in order to help her to her feet, but she shrugged him away, continuing to stare forward into the darkness. "Still I know that my God is beside me," she continued. "He will heal me and guide me. With him I'll be safe."

"Vera, I know you don't have any reason to trust me, but we have got to get off this mountain." He reached to take her hand. "God, you're like ice."

"God?" she laughed. "Whose God?"

He picked her up and carried her home.

Back in her house, Rafe lit a fire, pulled off her wet clothes, and bundled her in heavy blankets. He made her hot tea.

When she seemed to be getting some color back in her cheeks, Rafe knelt beside her.

"Vera, I know that you have no reason at all to believe me, to believe in me, but please listen to me. This may be the last opportunity I have to talk to you."

Vera continued to stare silently at the flames.

"I know that your religion tells you to turn the other cheek, and in time I hope that you will be able to forgive me for what I've taken from you."

"Scripture also says that you should 'shake the dust off your sandals' and leave those who are unreceptive to God's word."

Rafe looked at her, and then bowed his head and began crying.

Vera didn't move.

After a while, he raised his head from the armrest of her chair. "Maybe in time you will come to understand that what I say is true. Vera, I love you. I realized that shortly after you left the other day. My heart had been frozen, 'betrothed unto the enemy,' as you once quoted from a poem, but your love, your understanding of goodness must have seeped through somehow, because the chill is gone and I'm a new man. Again, I love you with everything I am, everything I have, everything I ever will be."

"What you are is nothing. You have nothing. You are ugly to me, Rafe."

He sat quietly beside her.

"I'm so glad that you feel love and happiness and fulfillment now, Rafe," she said sarcastically. "Because you have drained all of that from me." A tear formed in her eye, but did not drop to her cheek.

"I can understand your feelings, but I swear to you, Vera, I've changed."

"And what about your father, the 'God of Darkness,' as you call him?" she asked mockingly. "Or was that just a lie, an excuse to get rid of me?"

"No, it was the truth, but he is now no longer my father. I have left him, and denounced his ways. I have usurped his authority, my identity, my destiny, because of you, Vera. Now I only want to share your love, to reflect goodness and beauty as you do."

"'Did,'" she corrected him. "Rafe, I can't believe you have the nerve to expect me to believe anything you say to me ever again. I don't know what you want from me, because I have nothing left to give; everything I treasured is gone now, because you took it from me."

"I am so sorry, Vera. My greatest wish is that you and I would be able to share a life of love, an extension of God's love, together." He put his hand on the armrest of her chair. "But if we are forced to live our lives apart, then I hope that some day you will be able to use this misfortune to make you a stronger, better person."

"Now look who's rationalizing!" She gathered the blanket closer around her and turned toward the fire.

He took her hand. "In time, I hope that you will be able to forgive me, and realize that this final declaration of my love for you, and everything decent that you stand for, is genuine."

Vera fell asleep in front of the fire with Rafe holding her hand. She was too weak to move.

She awakened some time later to the sound of Rafe's voice. Startled, she looked around, trying to regain her bearings. It was still raining outside, and an occasional flash of lightning from the window illuminated Rafe kneeling on the floor, his eyes closed in prayer.

"Creator God," Rafe prayed, "Father of all fathers. I again ask your forgiveness for finding you so late in my life. Please forgive the damage and destruction I have caused others as a result of my sinful nature.

"Thank you for the gift of your love as expressed through your daughter, Vera. Through her, you were able to reach me, and warm my icy heart.

"Help me to follow her example. I give you myself, Lord, and everything good that I now believe in; please use my energy to strengthen Vera so that she may continue to do your work in this world.

"I pray that my joining you will make some difference in the balance of power between good and evil.

"I give you my life, Creator God, and am thankful that you have the grace to accept it. Amen."

Vera joined Rafe on the floor, on her knees. They looked at one another, silent tears streaming from their eyes.

Finally they embraced, the blanket falling from Vera's shoulders. Being naked now seemed natural, since they had both bared their souls.

She awakened in the morning to a stream of light shining through the window and to the sound of birds singing. Rafe was gone.

A few hours earlier, Rafe had begun his walk home in the darkness.

It had taken all of his resolve to leave Vera, who had been so sweetly sleeping in his arms, but it had been necessary to leave her in order to remove her from any threat of danger.

He smiled to himself as he remembered the loving tenderness she expressed as she surrendered herself to him.

His every instinct had screamed to stay with her, for forever. It seemed a cruel paradox that he must leave her in order to protect her. He hoped that some day she would understand.

The loving thoughts that captivated Rafe's mind seemed so intense as to be reflected in reality.

Rafe thought he heard the sound of soft laughter and noticed that the trees and shrubbery lining the lonely road almost seemed to be quietly repeating his very thoughts to him.

The breeze flickered through the leaves and seemed to whisper "I love you" and lightly rattled the wet branches, which echoed "Don't leave me." Rafe smiled at the words, Vera's thoughts, Rafe's thoughts, so strongly felt as to seem to resonate through nature.

Rafe's spine stiffened at the icy realization which then attacked his senses: these were his father's thoughts.

The darkness which surrounded him permeated his soul as he recognized the calling of a jealous, vengeful god in search of his lost son.

His charred body was discovered in his house. His death was a mystery, because nothing else in the house was burned or even scorched. Some surmised that he had been struck by lightning and then struggled into the house to die.

Rafe died as punishment for denouncing his evil origins, but his death had been a sacrifice, a victory for the forces of good.

Since no family of Rafe's could be discovered, the church that employed Vera assumed his burial expenses.

Vera attended the funeral. She still felt numb from all that she had experienced, and hoped that time would provide the context that would give Rafe's life, and death, meaning.

The minister read from the Book of Ecclesiastes, 3:1-8:

"For everything there is a season,
and a time for every matter under heaven:
a time to be born, and a time to die;
a time to plant, and a time to pluck up what is planted;
a time to kill, and a time to heal;

a time to break down, and a time to build up;
a time to weep, and a time to laugh;
a time to mourn, and a time to dance;
a time to throw away stones, and a time to gather stones together;
a time to embrace, and a time to refrain from embracing;
a time to seek, and a time to lose;
a time to keep, and a time to throw away;
a time to tear, and a time to sew;
a time to keep silence, and a time to speak;
a time to love, and a time to hate;
a time for war, and a time for peace."

Vera stood at the cemetery in the early morning hours, her hands clasped in front of her as she bowed her head in prayer. She didn't realize that beneath her hands, within her belly, a child, a life, the image of an unfulfilled destiny was forming.

Time alone would tell whether it would be a child of evil, conceived out of a need for domination, or a child of love, conceived after redemption . . . or perhaps, like all of us, a child who must struggle daily between the opposing forces on this continuum called life.